Look for these other
SpongeBob SquarePants
chapter books!

Stephen Hillenburg

Based on the TV series *SpongeBob SquarePants*®
created by Stephen Hillenburg as seen on Nickelodeon®

SIMON SPOTLIGHT
An imprint of Simon & Schuster Children's Publishing Division
1230 Avenue of the Americas, New York, New York 10020

Manufactured in the United States of America

First Edition
6 8 10 9 7

ISBN 0-689-84174-4

Library of Congress Control Number 00-133517

SpongeBob Superstar

by Annie Auerbach
illustrated by Mark O'Hare

Simon Spotlight/Nickelodeon

New York   London   Toronto   Sydney   Singapore

chapter one

"Hey, Patrick!" SpongeBob SquarePants called. "Come look at this!"

Patrick took another lick of his ice-cream cone. "What is it?" he asked, and made his way to his best friend.

"I picked this up at the Krusty Krab as I was leaving," SpongeBob explained and handed Patrick a flyer.

Patrick took the flyer and began to read:

Do you want to be a rich and famous star?

Do you dream of making it big in Celebrity Sea?

WELL, HERE'S YOUR CHANCE!
SEEKING THE UNDERWATER WORLD'S
BIGGEST DAREDEVIL FOR A TV SPECIAL.
AUDITIONS TOMORROW, 10 A.M.
AT THE KRUSTY KRAB
B.Y.O.S. (BRING YOUR OWN STUNT).

"A daredevil TV show!" exclaimed SpongeBob. "Do you know what this means?"

"Uh . . . must-see TV?" guessed Patrick.

SpongeBob grinned and replied, "Well, of course. But it *also* means we can show off our stunts. We could become famous!"

"But we don't have any stunts," said Patrick.

"Sure we do!" SpongeBob declared. "We just haven't thought of them yet. Hmmm . . . ."

"I can . . . I can . . . what can I do?" Patrick wondered.

SpongeBob thought for a moment. He looked at the melting ice cream in Patrick's hand. "You can do something with ice cream!" he told Patrick.

"But how is that a daredevil stunt?" Patrick asked.

"Uh . . . I know! What about the most number of licks it takes to finish an ice-cream cone?" SpongeBob suggested with a smile.

"Yeah!" cheered Patrick. "I'm a daredevil!"

"Well, I'd better go think of a stunt to practice," SpongeBob said. "I'll see you tomorrow."

"See you then!" Patrick called. "I'd better practice, too!" He began to lick and count, "One . . . two . . . three . . ."

SpongeBob went home. After he fed Gary, he took a bath and heated up a leftover Krabby Patty for dinner.

"Ooh . . ." he said, looking at the TV listings while he ate. "There's a *Mermaid Man and Barnacle Boy* marathon on tonight!" Then he remembered he was going to practice a stunt for tomorrow's daredevil auditions. "Well . . . I'll just watch one or two episodes and *then* I'll practice."

chapter two

The next thing SpongeBob knew, light was streaming in through the window. He yawned and rubbed his eyes. "Huh? It's morning already?" he wondered aloud. He saw that the television was still on. A newscaster was reciting the traffic report: "And expect big delays between Coral Boulevard and Anchor Way. Auditions for the World's Biggest Daredevil started at ten o'clock. It seems that everyone in Bikini Bottom is there. Good luck! This is Don Shell reporting . . ."

"Aaaahh!" SpongeBob screamed and sprang

up from the chair. He looked at the clock. "Oh, no! It's already eleven-thirty! I'm late!" He dove into his square pants and ran out the door.

☆

By the time SpongeBob made it to the Krusty Krab, there was a line that seemed to stretch for miles. There were wanna-be daredevils with all sorts of vehicles, gizmos, and gadgets—from inflatable water skis that fit an octopus's eight legs to a pair of stilts made from giant kelp.

"Oh, no! I didn't bring anything!" SpongeBob cried. He squeezed his way through, shouting, "Krusty Krab employee coming through!" He made it inside the Krusty Krab just in time to see Squidward's audition.

"I will be performing my favorite piece, Solitude in E Minor," Squidward announced and began to play his cherished clarinet.

A slimy, stocky fish sitting in a director's chair interrupted him. "Uh, hey! Excuse me?" he said. "Would you tell me how this is a stunt?"

Squidward was instantly offended. "Well, if you must know, it's not actually a stunt," Squidward confessed. "I figured once you heard my brilliant playing, you'd want to make a TV special around *me*."

"Next!" the director called in a gruff voice, his sharp teeth showing.

"You obviously don't know good talent when you see it!" Squidward replied.

"Well, if you get any, let me know," replied the director. Everyone laughed as Squidward slunk away.

SpongeBob put his name on the sign-up sheet and then spotted Patrick.

"I came by your house this morning," Patrick said, "but there was no answer."

"Yeah, I overslept," SpongeBob explained.

"Patrick Star?" an assistant called out.

SpongeBob gave his buddy a thumbs-up sign. Patrick grinned.

"So what stunt are you gonna do?" the director asked Patrick.

"I . . . uh . . . I . . . uh . . . I forget," Patrick replied nervously. He looked over and saw SpongeBob who was making funny faces with his tongue.

Patrick started to giggle. Then he understood what SpongeBob was doing. He looked down at the ice-cream cone in his hand and said, "Oh, yeah! I'm going to do an ice-cream stunt!"

"Oh, boy, this should be good," the director said sarcastically.

"I will attempt the most number of licks it takes to eat this ice-cream cone," explained Patrick. "One . . . two . . ."

Gulp!

"Two licks? What happened?" asked the director.

"Oops! I guess I was hungry," Patrick admitted.

"Well, you'll have plenty of time to eat ice cream—because you won't be on *this* TV special!" the director told him. He looked at his watch. "Everyone take five!"

SpongeBob walked over to Patrick. "Don't

worry about it," he said. "If I get picked and become rich and famous, I promise I'll buy you as much ice cream as you want."

"Thanks!" Patrick replied.

Just then SpongeBob saw his pal, Sandy.

"Howdy, SpongeBob," Sandy said. "Where ya been?"

SpongeBob tried to cover and explained, "Uh . . . I overslept . . . because I was up all night perfecting my stunt."

"Really?" replied Sandy. "I can't wait to see it!"

"Uh, yeah," said SpongeBob. "It should be, uh, interesting. Hey, did you already audition?"

"Sure did!" Sandy said. "I did my best karate tricks. The director really liked me. He said I could be a guest star in the TV special!"

"Way to go, Sandy!" SpongeBob told her.

"The director is still looking for the star, though," Sandy explained. "So you still have a shot!"

"Great!" said SpongeBob. But he knew he'd have to think up a magnificent stunt pretty quickly! "Excuse me, Sandy. I should, uh, go prepare."

"Break a leg!" said Sandy.

SpongeBob looked worried.

"It means good luck," Sandy explained with a laugh.

SpongeBob headed straight for the kitchen. He had to think of a stunt immediately. "Hi, Mr. Krabs," he said to his boss.

"Well, ahoy there, me boy," said Mr. Krabs.

"You're not auditioning, are you?" SpongeBob asked him.

Mr. Krabs laughed. "Oh, no," he said. "I made a deal with the director to use the Krusty Krab for auditions."

"And what do you get in exchange?" asked SpongeBob.

Mr. Krabs pulled out a wheelbarrow of cash. "All of this!" he said excitedly. "I just love those Celebrity Sea types!"

"Mr. Krabs, I need a favor," said SpongeBob.

"Sure, SpongeBob. What is it?" asked Mr. Krabs, counting his money.

"My stunt involves a spatula," SpongeBob explained, quickly looking around, "and Krabby Patties. Can I use the kitchen? Please? Please?"

Mr. Krabs wasn't really listening to SpongeBob. "Uh, sure, SpongeBob . . . seventy-eight dollars, seventy-nine dollars . . ."

SpongeBob grinned. Just then he heard his name being called. He raced out of the kitchen.

chapter three

"SpongeBob SquarePants?" an assistant called out again.

"That's me!" said a cheerful SpongeBob.

"What stunt are you going to perform?" the assistant asked.

"Follow me into the kitchen," SpongeBob said and led the way.

The director looked around at his crew. They were used to directing others, not being directed. Then he grimaced and said, "This better be good."

Once in the kitchen, SpongeBob did his best to

make his stunt sound daring and inventive. He announced, "I'm about to perform a stunt *never* attempted—right before your eyes." Deep down, SpongeBob knew that was really true since he hadn't prepared *anything*. "I shall attempt to make three hundred Krabby Patties in a row."

"How is that a stunt?" someone yelled.

"Boo!" hollered someone else.

SpongeBob noticed the director getting impatient. "You didn't let me finish," he said quickly. "I will perform this daring stunt blindfolded, over a hot-hot-hot grill, *and* with one hand tied behind my back—my Patty-flipping hand!"

"Oooh!" the audience gasped.

Once he was blindfolded and his award-winning flipping hand was tied behind his back, SpongeBob went to work. But because SpongeBob was nervous and he couldn't see what he was doing, he was making Krabby Patties inside out! The bun was on the inside, then the Krabby Patty, mustard, ketchup, pickle, onion, and tomato. The

lettuce was on the outside where the bun should have been!

Everyone started laughing.

"That must be jealous laughter to throw me off," SpongeBob thought to himself, still blindfolded. "I'll just work faster!" Unfortunately, his left hand just couldn't flip as precisely as his right hand, which was still tied behind his back. Soon he was flipping Krabby Patties all over the place.

The director and his crew all covered their heads. It seemed to be raining Krabby Patties!

Just then Mr. Krabs walked in. "What the barnacle!" he cried. "Me kitchen! Me Krabby Patties!" He ran over to SpongeBob who was buried beneath a pile of Krabby Patties and took off his blindfold.

By this time, everyone was hysterical—even the director. He didn't know which was funnier: the stunt or SpongeBob himself. He pulled his production team close to him. "Forget the daredevil stunt show," he whispered with a sinister laugh. "I've got an idea that will make us millionaires! We're going to turn this show into a rip-roaring blooper show. We'll be the funniest thing on television!"

The director called SpongeBob over. "Hey, kid, what's your name?"

"SpongeBob SquarePants," replied the harried fry cook.

The director stuck his fin out. "I'm Cuda. Barry Cuda," he said.

"It's an honor, sir," SpongeBob replied, shaking his fin.

"How would you like to be a star?" the director asked SpongeBob.

"Me?" asked SpongeBob.

"That's right. You're the next daredevil superstar!" Barry Cuda assured him. "There won't be an invertebrate in Bikini Bottom who won't want to be in your shoes!"

"Woo-hoo!!" SpongeBob exclaimed.

Barry immediately saw that SpongeBob was

easily influenced. "That will make it easier to get him to do what I want," he muttered to himself. Then he pulled out a floor-length contract and said, "Okay, let's make a deal!"

SpongeBob couldn't believe it. "I'm going to be a star! SpongeBob SquarePants is gonna be a *star*!" he said dreamily to no one in particular.

"That's right," Barry assured him. "A star is born! In fact, just like a real star, I think you need a stage name—how about SpongeBob Superstar?"

SpongeBob practically jumped for joy as he signed the contract—with his new celebrity name.

"Everyone go home!" Barry Cuda announced. "We've found our star!"

SpongeBob beamed. He ran over to his friends and excitedly said, "Can you believe it? *Me!* He picked little ol' *me* to be the star!"

"Way to go, little square dude!" Sandy told him.

"That's me boy!" Mr. Krabs said, patting him on the back.

"I just can't believe it!" SpongeBob shouted.

"Wow!" cried Patrick. "I know a *real* superstar! Can I touch you?"

SpongeBob stuck out his hand and grinned. "*Almost* a superstar. But when I become rich and famous, I promise I'll share everything with you!"

Squidward, though, was still annoyed about the clarinet incident and said, "Well, at least you won't be working *here* for a while."

"Oh, no! I forgot!" SpongeBob exclaimed. "Mr. Krabs, is it okay if I take some time off to tape this special?"

"Absolutely!" Mr. Krabs replied. "I'm sure Squidward won't mind covering your shifts," he added with a belly laugh.

"Argh!" Squidward groaned.

Barry Cuda approached SpongeBob and told him, "Shooting starts tomorrow morning."

"Oh, Mr. Cuda," began SpongeBob, "these are my friends."

"Yeah, whatever," said Barry. "See you tomorrow."

"Should I practice any stunts?" asked SpongeBob.

"NO!" Barry said a little too quickly. "I mean, uh, no, it's not necessary."

"Okay, Mr. Cuda," SpongeBob replied cheerily. "See you tomorrow!"

chapter four

The next day SpongeBob woke up bright and early. He was so excited. "Superstar! Superstar!" he sang eagerly as he left his pineapple house.

The first stunt was to take place in Oyster Bay. The set was buzzing with activity everywhere SpongeBob looked. Set decorators were dressing up the set. Lighting technicians were adjusting lights. Costumers were putting the finishing touches on costumes.

"So this is what showbiz is all about," SpongeBob said in awe.

Barry, the director, spotted the one-of-a-kind creature who was going to make him a millionaire. "SpongeBob! Come over here, kid. Time for makeup and wardrobe," Barry told him.

"Aye, aye, Mr. Cuda!" said SpongeBob with a salute.

"Call me Barry," the director told him.

"Aye, aye, Barry!" SpongeBob replied.

Three long hours later, SpongeBob was ready. The daredevil costume originally designed wasn't made for a sponge—let alone a square one. Needless to say, a lot of sewing took place that morning.

Finally SpongeBob emerged wearing a pair of square trunks and a matching cape, and holding a shiny helmet. "I don't know," he worried, pointing to the costume. "Is it really me?"

"Maybe not," replied Barry. "But it *is* SpongeBob Superstar!"

"Oh, yeah!" agreed SpongeBob, his eyes lighting up.

SpongeBob's first stunt involved trying to get the rare black pearl from the granddaddy of all oysters, The Big Kahuna.

When SpongeBob was first told of this stunt he said, "Seems easy enough! I'm sure that Mr. Kahuna won't mind if I borrow his pearl." What SpongeBob didn't realize was what he'd have to go through to retrieve the pearl. With a bright red skateboard, SpongeBob was supposed to skate on a track through the oyster bed. The track leading up to the prized pearl was full of nail-biting turns, extreme loop-de-loops, and hair-raising drops! As if that weren't scary enough, swimming below the oyster bed were twenty electric eels!

After SpongeBob found out what he was supposed to do, his eyes popped out of his head. Once he recovered, he cried, "I'm gonna do what?" his head shrinking slightly in fear.

"Everyone's gotta start somewhere," Barry reminded him.

"But what about those eels?" SpongeBob asked. "One electric shock and I'll . . . I'll . . . I'll be all dried up!"

"You can do it, kiddo," Barry urged him. "This is your first step toward stardom, remember?"

SpongeBob's head swelled up a bit and he grabbed his helmet. "You're right. Let's do it!"

Barry wouldn't let SpongeBob do any practice runs, stating that he wanted to capture the excitement and drama of doing it for the very first time.

Once SpongeBob was in place, Barry yelled, "Action!" and the cameras started to roll.

SpongeBob started skateboarding down the track and completed the first turn. Unfortunately, it was feeding time for the electric eels, and SpongeBob looked like the perfect lunch to them.

"Stay back! Stay back!" SpongeBob shouted at the eels. "You wouldn't like me anyway! I'm kind of chewy!" But the eels were still coming at him. He started to skate even faster. Then, on a loop-de-loop, something caught his eye inside one of the oysters. It was the most beautiful black pearl he had ever seen.

Crash! Boing! Boing! The skateboard went flying off the track as SpongeBob fell and bounced off a row of oysters.

"Whoa!" SpongeBob yelled as he tumbled up and around, the eels nipping at him along the way. Finally he ended up headfirst inside of an oyster—the one that held that precious black pearl. "I've got it!" he mumbled.

"Cut!" yelled Barry.

Luckily, SpongeBob was just out of reach of the eels, but with only his feet sticking out of the oyster, he was still worried. That certainly *wasn't* the way the stunt was supposed to go, was it?

After the production crew rescued SpongeBob, Barry rushed right over to him and raved, "Fantastic!"

"Huh?" said SpongeBob.

"You really nailed it, kid," Barry told him.

"But I wasn't supposed to—" began SpongeBob.

"Eh, don't worry about it. That was better than we could have ever planned!" Barry declared and signaled his crew.

"Uh . . . gee, thanks," SpongeBob said hesitantly.

The crew surrounded SpongeBob and applauded. "That was great! You're so brave! You're a star!" they all cooed.

SpongeBob shrugged. "Well, maybe it wasn't as bad as I thought," he said, and again his head swelled up a little.

On his way home, SpongeBob ran into Patrick.

"How was your first day?" Patrick asked excitedly.

"It was incredible!" exclaimed SpongeBob. "I think I might be a natural at this daredevil stuff!"

"Holy sea cow!" cried Patrick. "My best friend's a daredevil star!"

All the way home, Patrick and SpongeBob planned what they'd do when SpongeBob became a big star.

chapter five

The following day, SpongeBob's daredevil stunts were to take place in Goo Lagoon. This time, SpongeBob wasn't afraid. He was ready to take on whatever stunts were assigned. After going through makeup and wardrobe, he sat and waited while final technical adjustments were made.

"SpongeBob, me boy!" a voice said.

SpongeBob jumped up. "Mr. Krabs!"

"I came to see how you're holding up," Mr. Krabs said. "I even brought you some Krabby Patties."

SpongeBob took a step back and replied, "Not

for me, thanks. I'm on a strict diet. A superstar's diet. No Krabby Patties allowed."

"Why, that's crazy!" Mr. Krabs exclaimed.

"It's a sacrifice we stars *must* make," SpongeBob said snootily. It was hard for him to concentrate, though, with the scent of Krabby Patties wafting through the air. They sure were tempting!

Mr. Krabs looked puzzled. "All right, lad, if you say so," he said. Then he quickly left because he suddenly felt out of place.

Barry came up to SpongeBob. "Ready for today's stunts?" he asked.

"You bet!" SpongeBob declared. Then after a moment he asked, "Uh, Barry? What *are* today's stunts?"

"They'll be a snap for you. Why, with your talent—and that face—I see big things in your future, SpongeBob! Now come on, surf's up!"

SpongeBob imagined his life in Celebrity Sea. All the money he could want, surrounded by adoring fans, getting asked for autographs . . .

His daydream was interrupted as he found himself being carried over to a surfboard. "Huh? I don't surf," SpongeBob said and looked around him.

"Aaahh!" he suddenly yelled. He was indeed on a surfboard. But he learned that he was supposed to surf on one foot, juggle ten plates, balance a stack of coral on his head, *and* balance a spoon on his nose—all at the same time!

"This isn't surfing!" he objected.

"Sure it is! It's surfing—SpongeBob Superstar-style!" replied Barry.

Before SpongeBob could protest any further, he was pushed out to Goo Lagoon by the production crew.

In typical SpongeBob fashion, the stunt didn't go at all the way it was meant to. A big wave swelled and SpongeBob panicked.

Crash! Splash!

Everything he was trying to balance went flying in different directions.

"Yikes!" he yelled. The enormous wave was

coming right at him. Not knowing what else to do, SpongeBob decided to try bodysurfing instead. He dropped onto his stomach and started to paddle with his hands. He felt like he was getting sucked into the wave so he began to paddle even faster. In fact, SpongeBob was paddling so fast that his arms became a whirlwind of motion, like propellers on an airplane. He desperately hoped that it would help save him.

But the only thing it did was cause the big wave to swell up even more, until it was almost a tidal wave!

"Whoa!" shouted SpongeBob as he actually began surfing the wave.

"Now that's what I call surfing!" an assistant remarked.

"And that's what I call comedy!" said Barry. "Keep rolling!"

Splash!

SpongeBob, the surfboard, and tons of water washed up onto the shore.

Barry didn't care. He couldn't have imagined a funnier stunt if he had thought of it himself! He whispered to his crew, "Make sure you help feed his ego." Then he approached SpongeBob. "What a star performance that was! You're great, kid!" Barry told him.

Once again, SpongeBob's head swelled up a bit. "Yeah, maybe I am . . ." He noticed the round of applause he was getting. Then his head swelled even more. "Yes! Yes! I *am* great!"

"We're losing light," said Barry. "Does our Superstar need a break, or can he do one more?"

"I'm ready! I'm ready!" SpongeBob declared, his head growing even larger.

"Excellent," said Barry. "Now where's that squirrel?"

Sandy came on to the set and announced, "Here I am, Mr. Cuda. I'm ready for my close-up."

"Very funny," Barry said with a sneer. "Now, this next stunt involves karate—"

"Oh, wow! I love karate!" SpongeBob

exclaimed, and he pulled out his safety gear. "Safety first!" He noticed his helmet was a little tighter than usual, but he could still squeeze it on.

"Hi-yah!" Sandy shouted, striking a position.

"Wah!" yelled SpongeBob with a spin.

SpongeBob and Sandy loved to practice karate. Barry tried his best not to get annoyed. After all, if his TV show was a success, he could retire to the hills of Celebrity Sea and spend his time counting his millions. "My little stars, why don't you save it for the camera, hmmm?"

Finally SpongeBob and Sandy were poised and ready for combat. They were to fight each other while jumping across dangerous Rock Falls. Rock Falls was made up of separate pieces of rock, each with a one-thousand-foot drop. One slip and it was into the wild blue yonder.

"Action!" called Barry.

"Prepare for a long, merciless whopping!" Sandy said confidently.

"That'll be the day!" SpongeBob replied.

"Hi-yah!" yelled Sandy as she did a powerful jump kick. She landed on SpongeBob's rock.

But SpongeBob was quick on his feet. He pulled out his best move: a double overhand squirrel-knot.

Sandy blocked it and jumped to another rock. "Nice try, Sponge Brain!" she said with a laugh.

Soon it became clear that Sandy was winning, which was unacceptable to SpongeBob. "After all, *I'm* the star," he said to himself.

As a last resort, SpongeBob used the best defense he could. With all his might, he took his huge head and pummeled Sandy with it. SpongeBob's head was now so large that it nearly threw him off balance—and off the steep rock!

Sandy seemed to be down when suddenly she squirmed out from underneath SpongeBob's head. With a loud "Wah!" she delivered a lethal knuckle punch.

SpongeBob flipped over and ended up facedown with his head wedged between two rocks.

"Cut!" yelled Barry. "Great job, you guys!"

Once SpongeBob was back on his feet, he pulled Sandy aside. He was very upset. "Did you *have* to do that last move?" he hissed. "You made me look bad out there!"

Sandy couldn't believe what she was hearing and quickly blurted out, "You didn't need me to help you look like a fool. You did that all by yourself. I won fair and square."

"It's not cool to steal the star's spotlight," SpongeBob said bitterly.

"I thought we were partners," said Sandy, "but I guess with your new stardom, there's not enough room for me. See ya, SpongeBob."

SpongeBob sighed. Sandy was one of his favorite pals. However, there wasn't much time to feel bad as Barry rushed over.

"What's the matter?" Barry asked.

"Sandy and I had a fight," SpongeBob explained. "I can't believe how stupid she made me look out there."

"Stupid? What are you, crazy?" replied Barry. "You were terrific, kid! Wait until you see the footage. *Trust me.*"

SpongeBob had no reason not to trust Barry. As his head swelled some more, he shrugged and said, "Sandy just doesn't understand show business, I guess."

"That's right! Tomorrow we'll shoot the last stunt. I'll see you then, Superstar," Barry called over his shoulder as he walked away.

"I'll be there!" SpongeBob promised.

chapter six

The next day when SpongeBob walked on to the set, he made a few heads turn. By now he was used to this, for he was a big star. He had already hired a press agent, a driver, and a personal secretary.

This time, however, heads were turning because SpongeBob's head had now swelled to epic proportions. Someone hesitantly pointed out the bizarre big-head phenomenon to Barry. But instead of getting mad, Barry just grinned. He quickly called a crew meeting.

"Now listen," he told everyone, "it appears

that SpongeBob's head is actually growing because of his big ego. I think his huge head will make this TV show even better. But we don't want him to become worried about it—you know how actors can be. So just act as if nothing's wrong."

"Sure!" replied the crew.

SpongeBob came out of the makeup and wardrobe departments feeling quite good about himself.

Barry began to explain to SpongeBob what the final stunt was. "Okay, Superstar, this is the most dangerous stunt yet. Only a *true* daredevil could pull it off."

"Bring it on!" declared SpongeBob. "I'm unstoppable!"

"Great! How do you like paddle bikes?" asked Barry.

"Love 'em!" SpongeBob exclaimed, though he had never been on one in his life.

"You are going to do a stunt that will not only be the most significant stunt for the TV show, but will surely put you in the record books, too!"

"All right!" SpongeBob cheered. "Hey, do I get paid extra for that?"

"Uh . . . we'll talk about that later," Barry said. "Now get on that paddle bike, Superstar, and let's make TV history!"

Sitting high atop a paddle bike at the edge of Jellyfish Fields, SpongeBob was supposed to ride down a ramp and jump over twenty-five boats lined up in a canyon below.

SpongeBob tried to put on his helmet, but it seemed to be way too small. After a few minutes of pushing and squishing, he barely got it around his head. He signaled to the crew that he was ready to go and the cameras began to roll. SpongeBob confidently started down the ramp.

Suddenly his helmet snapped off and fell over the edge of the ramp. "Oh, no!" SpongeBob worried. But soon he'd be worrying about something else.

Buzz . . . buzz . . . buzz . . .

"What's that sound?" Barry wondered.

Buzz . . . buzz . . . buzz . . .

SpongeBob was gaining speed.

BUZZ . . . BUZZ . . . BUZZ . . .

The entire crew looked up in horror. Following SpongeBob down the ramp was a huge group of jellyfish! The leader appeared to be wearing a helmet—the helmet SpongeBob had dropped!

BUZZ . . . BUZZ . . . BUZZ . . .

SpongeBob finally looked behind him. "Yeeooooww!" he shrieked, and lost his balance.

Screech!

The paddle bike went careening off the ramp and into the canyon. Flying through the air, SpongeBob separated from the bike and landed in one of the boats below. Luckily, his huge head cushioned the fall! SpongeBob turned himself right side up in the boat, put his foot on the gas, and floored it. He raced through the area, still followed by a gang of angry jellyfish.

"Ow! Ow!" cried the crew members as they were stung by the jellyfish.

But with only his career on his mind, Barry ordered, "Keep rolling!"

SpongeBob steered the boat out of the canyon, hoping he would lose the jellyfish. But they followed him all the way through Goo Lagoon and even into Bikini Bottom, stinging everyone along the way. To make matters worse, SpongeBob still didn't have his driver's license, so he was hitting nearly everything in his zigzagging path.

Finally SpongeBob was able to circle around and end up back in Jellyfish Fields. Just then, he had an idea. He called to Barry, "Play some music! It's our only chance!"

Someone quickly turned on a boom box and suddenly the jellyfish became calmer and all moved to the beat of the music.

"Cut! That's a wrap!" called Barry. "Thank you everyone!"

No one reacted with the joy normally experienced at the end of a TV shoot. Instead, they were all groaning and nursing their painful stings.

As SpongeBob got out of the boat, he noticed that he had survived with no stings at all. "I guess that's my protective star-coating," he said to himself. "I knew I was a natural daredevil."

"SpongeBob!" called a voice.

SpongeBob whirled around to see Patrick standing there. "Did you see it, Patrick? Did you see that amazing stunt?"

"Uh-huh!" replied Patrick. "*Everyone* in Bikini Bottom did! The hospitals are overflowing!"

"I'm glad they all could be a part of my rising success," said SpongeBob.

Patrick was about to ask SpongeBob what he meant when Barry came over.

Barry looked at Patrick and said, "Well, well, well, if it isn't the ice-cream king." He snickered and looked at SpongeBob to join in.

SpongeBob laughed too, which surprised Patrick. Why would his best friend laugh at him, he wondered.

"Well, Superstar," Barry said, "I'll see you at

the premiere. Invite whoever you want."

"Wow! My first premiere!" gloated SpongeBob.

"Hey, SpongeBob, why don't we celebrate?" suggested Patrick. "We could go get ice cream or something."

SpongeBob scoffed. "I don't have time for those trivial things," he told Patrick. "I've got interviews to give, people to meet, places to go . . ."

"But what about all the plans we made for when you were a big star?" Patrick said, feeling hurt.

But SpongeBob didn't notice. "Uh, yeah . . . we'll do lunch. Have your secretary call my secretary," he replied snottily.

"But I don't have a secretary!" called Patrick as SpongeBob walked out, talking on his new shell phone.

chapter seven

Finally it was the night of the TV special world premiere. Besides being broadcast oceanwide, Barry had rented out a theater for a celebrity-filled screening. It was a star-studded event! Stars and celebrities from far and deep showed up, including actor Albert Albatross, comedian Lainie Angelfish, famed writer Harriet Herring, and the always magnificent Catfish van Damsel. Even Lady Beluga was there with her stunning daughter, Caviar!

By this time, SpongeBob's ego was so big that he could hardly fit his head through the door. He was so excited to be seeing his name and sponginess on-screen. SpongeBob walked down the red carpet, and photographers snapped his picture as he posed and signed autographs. He was more than ready to embrace his fans and his newfound stardom as a famous daredevil.

Inside the theater, the screening was about to begin. SpongeBob looked around. All the seats he had saved for his friends were empty. "Where could they be?" he wondered. He knew his secretary had sent out invitations to all the little people in Bikini Bottom.

"I'm sure they'll be here soon," SpongeBob said. Eventually the lights dimmed and his friends still weren't there. "Well, their loss," he mumbled, trying to convince himself.

The music cued up and a voice-over was heard: "From the famous fish that brought you *When Anchovies Attack II,* comes the first in a series of daredevil specials." A title graphic flashed on the screen.

SpongeBob's eyes bugged out. The TV special was no longer called *Underwater World's Biggest Daredevil.* It was changed to *Underwater World's Biggest Goofball!*

The director had tricked him! Watching the first stunt, SpongeBob slumped down in his seat. It was no longer a TV special about daredevil stunts, but about stunts gone hysterically wrong. He had made such a fool of himself! Totally embarrassed, SpongeBob's swollen head actually began to shrink.

SpongeBob could only bear to watch about half of the show. Completely humiliated, he slunk out of his seat and out of the theater.

As SpongeBob walked through the streets of Bikini Bottom, he passed houses where families were watching the TV special. He could hear them roaring with laughter and his head shrank some more.

Up ahead, SpongeBob spotted the Krusty Krab. He felt a glimmer of hope. He rushed up to

the window and pressed his face against the glass. "Hey! What are all my friends doing here? They were supposed to be at my premiere. Well, only one way to find out," he said and went inside.

From all the laughter, it seemed that everyone was having a pretty good time. SpongeBob quickly looked around to see if it was because of his embarrassing TV show, but he didn't see a television. They just seemed to be having fun.

"Hi, everybody!" SpongeBob shouted.

But no one answered him.

"Wasn't that a great day at Goo Lagoon today?" Patrick said to Sandy.

"It sure was!" declared Sandy.

"You went to Goo Lagoon without me?" SpongeBob asked Patrick. But Patrick just turned the other way.

"Mr. Krabs, that was the best Krabby Patty I've ever had," Squidward stated.

"Are there any Krabby Patties left?" asked SpongeBob, feeling quite hungry.

Mr. Krabs just ignored him and said, "Why, thank you, Squidward! Just for that, remind me to give you a promotion."

Squidward's eyes lit up and he replied, "Uh, Mr. Krabs? Give me a promotion."

The group broke out into hysterical laughter.

"Ha ha ha ha!" SpongeBob joined in.

Suddenly everyone else became quiet. SpongeBob's head shrank some more.

"In fact, I think there's an opening for a fry cook," Mr. Krabs continued.

"Wait!" SpongeBob cried. "That's *my* job!"

Still, no one was listening to him.

"Remember the good ol' days when SpongeBob was the fry cook?" asked Patrick.

"Yeah," agreed Squidward. "Now he's just a legend in his own mind."

Everyone chuckled. By this time, SpongeBob's head not only had shrunk back to its normal size, but it had begun to shrink even smaller. Defeated, he headed into the kitchen and began to sob.

"What have I done?" he moaned. "I've made a fool of myself on oceanwide TV *and* lost all my friends." He dabbed his eyes with some seaweed. "No TV deal is worth losing all of this. I don't belong in Celebrity Sea; I belong right here in Bikini Bottom!"

Brrrriinnggg!

SpongeBob's shell phone was ringing. "Hello?" he said sheepishly.

It was Barry Cuda. He was *not* happy. "Where are you, kid? Why aren't you *here?*"

SpongeBob began to sob again. He squeaked out, "I'm at the Krusty Krab."

"I'll be right there," Barry told him.

A few minutes later, Barry burst through the front door of the Krusty Krab. He didn't greet anyone. He just demanded, "Where's Superstar?"

SpongeBob's friends hated that name. With hisses, they all pointed to the kitchen.

"I'm sorry, Barry," SpongeBob said when Barry came into the kitchen.

"Sorry ain't gonna cut it, Superstar," said Barry. "You're under contract. You *have* to talk to the press and go to the parties. I thought that this was what you wanted!"

SpongeBob mustered up all his courage and said, "I wanted you to make me a star—not a fool!"

"Hey, come on. This is show business, kid," Barry said. "It's a fish-eat-fish world out there."

"Well, I'm *not* a fish and I want out of your fish-eat-fish world," SpongeBob declared. "I want to go back to my normal life—where I can be with my friends, and go jellyfishing, and go bubble blowing—"

Like the sleazy director he was, Barry whipped out the contract SpongeBob had signed. "Don't make me show my teeth, Superstar," said Barry. "You're all mine for the next ten years."

"What?" exclaimed SpongeBob. "Let me see that!" He grabbed the contract and read the really, really, really fine print. He sighed and said, "Uh-oh."

Just then SpongeBob's friends burst into the kitchen. They had overheard the entire conversation. Even though SpongeBob had been annoying lately, they sure weren't going to let this barracuda bully him.

"Let me see that contract," said Mr. Krabs. "Hmm . . . very interesting . . ."

"What?" Barry said, growing impatient.

"This contract is between you and SpongeBob Superstar," Mr. Krabs explained. "But there's no one here by that name."

"He's standing right there," said Barry, pointing to SpongeBob.

"No, I'm SpongeBob *SquarePants,*" SpongeBob corrected him.

"So this contract isn't legal," Mr. Krabs pointed out.

"But . . . but . . ." began Barry, getting very frustrated. "This is not the end of this. I'm talking to my lawyers!" Then he stormed out.

"I just hate those Celebrity Sea types!" Mr. Krabs declared.

SpongeBob felt grateful and gushed, "You guys didn't have to come and rescue me—but I'm *so* glad you did!"

"We knew you needed help," said Sandy.

"I think you needed rescuing from yourself," Squidward said.

"Yeah, I guess I did get a little out of control, huh?" said SpongeBob.

Everyone just stared at him.

"Okay, okay, I got *a lot* out of control," he admitted. "I'm really sorry."

"That's okay. You're forgiven," everyone told him.

"I can't believe I was going to give up *all* this for a life in Celebrity Sea," said SpongeBob.

"All what?" asked Patrick.

"All of my good friends," answered SpongeBob.

"And Krabby Patties!" added Mr. Krabs. He handed SpongeBob a spatula. "Welcome back, SpongeBob! It hasn't been the same without you."

"It's good to be home," said SpongeBob and he fired up the grill. He was happy to be back and happy his head was back to its normal square size—just the perfect size.